FRANKIE!
FRANKIE...

WORDS AND PICTURES BY
MATHEW FRANKLIN

Frankie's Scared of Everything

Building Block Press
Louisville, KY
www.buildingblockpress.com

ISBN: 978-1-944201-22-7

First Edition.

KIE'S

SCARED OF EVERYTHING

NO SLEEP FOR FRANKIE.

GOOD NIGHT, FRANKIE.

HIS MIND RACES
AND THE THOUGHTS START SNEAKING...

SCREECH

IT SOUND LIKE A ROBOT
CRASHING
CREEEAKIN

AN ESCAPE ROUTE AHEAD!
DOWN THE STAIRS TO THE KITCHEN.

AWAY FROM THIS ROBOTS' SNATCHING,
BUT OH NO!!

It sounds like
a dino
scraping,
scratching

IT'S TIME TO GO!
WHIPFL
...AND FRANKIE'S GOT MOVES.

FLIP FLIP
WEEEEE
OHHHHHH
BUT OH NO!!
OUT THE DOOR HE GOES SAILING.

IT SOUNDS LIKE A SEA CREATURE
WAILING, FLAILING

ONLY ONE PLACE TO GO.
THE DEEP DEEP BASEMENT.

GOTTA GET AWAY FROM THE CREATURE LOOMING!
WOOSH
WOOSH
WOOSH
WOOSH
BUT OH NO!!

IT SOUNDS LIKE
A
MOLE-MAN
FUMING,
BOOMING

WITH HIS OPTIONS GONE, WHAT IS FRANKIE TO DO?
AHH! HE KNOWS... OFF TO MOM'S ROOM!

MOM'S Room

MOM! MY MIND IS RACING. YOU'RE MY ONLY HOPE!
OH FRANKIE. IMAGINATION CAN BE A SLIPPERY SLOPE.

THE WASHING MACHINE BANGS AND "BOOMS".
A CAR ALARM OUTSIDE WAILS AND SCREAMS.

THE ICE MACHINE IN THE KITCHEN, SCRAPES AND SCRATCHES.
THE TRAIN OUTSIDE YOUR WINDOW CRASHES AND CREAKS!!

THE MACHINES IN THIS WORLD
ALL THE INVENTIONS YOU HEAR,
BEGAN IN SOMEONE'S HEAD
JUST LIKE YOUR FEARS.
YOU MAY BE SCARED NOW
BUT SOON YOU WILL SEE,
YOUR IMAGINATION IS THE GREATEST
GIFT THERE CAN BE.

SO TAKE YOUR IDEAS, AND MAKE SOMETHING NEW.
YOUR FEARS CAN BE FRIENDS, IT'S ALL UP TO YOU!

FRANKIE
FRANKIE!

FRANKIE!
FRANKIE!

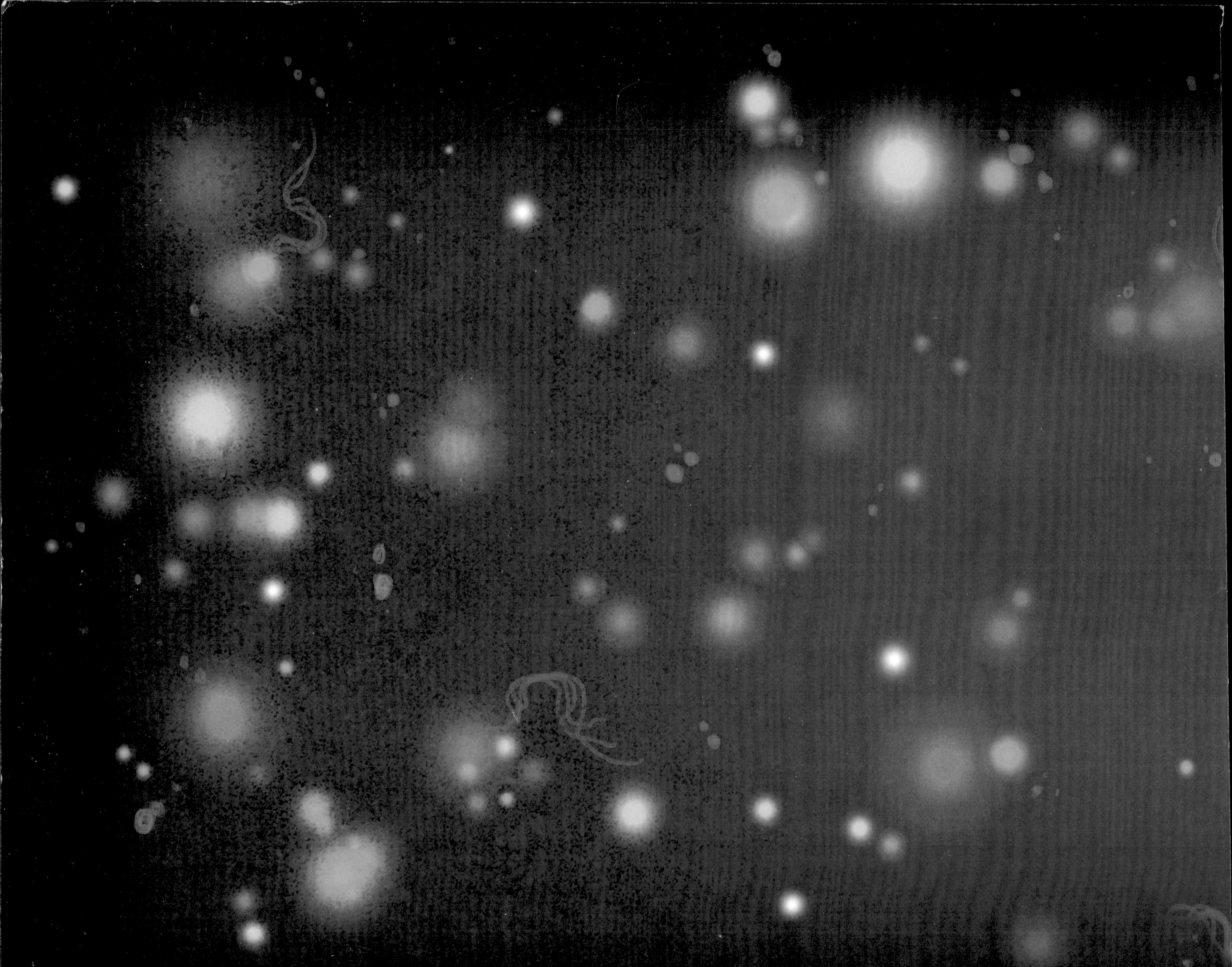